Batty and Catty

By Joe Rhatigan

Illustrated by James Rey Sanchez

Catty lived in a very fine home.

Batty lived up high in a tree.

One afternoon, they bragged to
each other.

Catty said, "You should be more like me!"

"I can leap high in the air,"
said Catty.

Batty smiled with a sigh.

"I don't need to leap at all,"
he said.
"I can spread my wings and fly."

"You can't balance on this fence,"
said Catty.
"You would fall down to the ground."

Batty flipped over and replied,
"Did you know that I sleep
upside down?"

Catty said, "I'm adorable, and people love me.
I have long whiskers and eyes that gleam."

Batty frowned and said,
"People are afraid of me.
They sometimes run away
and scream."

Batty started crying.
Catty knew that bragging
was not nice.

She said, "What if we teach each other something we like to do? I can show you how to chase mice!"

Batty taught Catty how to sing.

Catty showed Batty how to sit
on laps.

Batty showed Catty how to hang
upside down.

And from that day forward...

that's how they took all their naps!

Consultant

Doug Dalton, M.A.Ed.
Elementary Teacher
Sierra Sands Unified School District, California

Publishing Credits

Rachelle Cracchiolo, M.S.Ed., *Publisher*
Emily R. Smith, M.A.Ed., *VP of Content Development*
Véronique Bos, *Creative Director*

Image Credits:
Illustrated by James Rey Sanchez

Library of Congress Cataloging-in-Publication Data

Names: Rhatigan, Joe, author. | Sanchez, James Rey, illustrator.
Title: Batty and Catty / by Joe Rhatigan ; illustrated by James Rey
  Sanchez.
Description: Huntington Beach, CA : Teacher Created Materials, [2022] |
  Includes book group questions. | Audience: Grades K-1.
Identifiers: LCCN 2020006402 (print) | LCCN 2020006403 (ebook) | ISBN
  9781087601304 (paperback) | ISBN 9781087619347 (ebook)
Subjects: LCSH: Readers (Primary) | Stories in rhyme. | Cats--Juvenile
  fiction. | Bats--Juvenile fiction.
Classification: LCC PE1119 .R46 2020 (print) | LCC PE1119 (ebook) | DDC
  428.6/2--dc23
LC record available at https://lccn.loc.gov/2020006402
LC ebook record available at https://lccn.loc.gov/2020006403

5482 Argosy Avenue
Huntington Beach, CA 92649
www.tcmpub.com
ISBN 978-1-0876-0130-4